"Mum! Dad! Over here!" Emily whispered.

"Oh my goodness!" her mum breathed as they looked at the scene before them. It was the perfect picture. On the other side of the bamboo there was a clearing and in that clearing sat a giant panda, her legs outstretched in front of her as she stripped the leaves off a stalk of bamboo.

"Don't look now but—" Emily's dad put his hand on her arm.

Emily gasped as a cub came ambling round from behind its mum with a rolling side-to-side gait. It opened its mouth and made a bleating noise again.

Meet all of Emily's
WILD FRIENDS

WILD FRIENDS
PANDA PLAYTIME

By Linda Chapman and Michelle Misra

Illustrated by Rob McPhillips

RED FOX

WWF WILD FRIENDS: PANDA PLAYTIME

A RED FOX BOOK 978 1 849 41692 4

First Published in Great Britain by Red Fox,
an imprint of Random House Children's Publishers UK
A Random House Group Company

This edition published 2012

1 3 5 7 9 10 8 6 4 2

MIX
Paper from
responsible sources
FSC® C016897

Set in Bembo MT
Red Fox Books are published by Random House Children's Publishers UK,
61–63 Uxbridge Road, London W5 5SA

www.**randomhousechildrens**.co.uk
www.**randomhouse**.co.uk

Addresses for companies within The Random House Group Limited
can be found at: www.randomhouse.co.uk/offices.htm

THE RANDOM HOUSE GROUP Limited Reg. No. 954009

A CIP catalogue record for this book is available from the British Library.

Printed and bound by CPI Group (UK) Ltd, Croydon, CR0 4YY

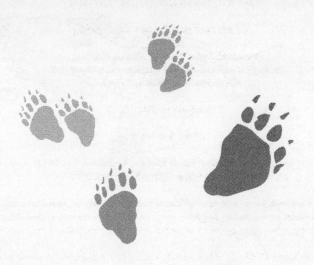

**Turn to page 77 for lots
of information on WWF,
plus some cool activities!**

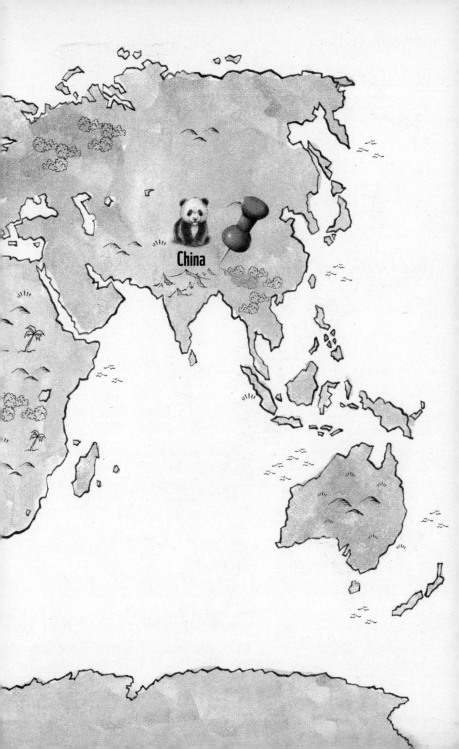

Exciting News!

Emily rested her pencil on the desk.
The other children at her table were still
copying the map of Great Britain from the
whiteboard at the front of the classroom.
Pushing her dark brown hair behind her
ears, Emily took a piece of scrap paper
and began to draw a panda. She sketched
a round body and head, coloured the little
ears in black and drew dark circles around
the eyes. She then added a stick of bamboo
in the panda's paws. She was concentrating
so hard she jumped when she heard her
teacher's voice behind her.

"Hmm," said Miss Haynes. "Pandas, Emily? I'm not sure *they're* found wild in the British Isles."

Emily blushed guiltily. "Sorry, Miss Haynes. It's just that I'm going to see them with my mum and dad in the summer holidays – in the mountains of China." Excitement bubbled up through her as she thought of what her parents had told her that morning before school.

Everyone on Emily's table looked surprised. The only person who didn't was Molly, Emily's best friend. Emily had told her the news as soon as she had got in.

"Oh wow! You're going to China?" said Anna across the table.

"Cool!" said Ben.

Miss Haynes clapped her hands for silence. "Everyone, take a break from your maps for a moment. This is very exciting news – Emily's going to China in the holidays. So, are your mum and dad going there because of work, Emily?"

Emily nodded. "They work for WWF . . ."

"WWF is an organization that helps endangered animals and protects the natural world," Miss Haynes explained for anyone who didn't know. "Your mother's a wildlife photographer, isn't she?"

"Yes, and Dad writes articles for the annual newsletter and gets involved with setting up projects," Emily finished. "They've been asked to go to China for a week, although I'm not quite sure why."

"What an adventure!" Miss Haynes went to the computer and, with a bit of quick typing and a few clicks of the mouse, she got the WWF website up on the whiteboard and went to the giant panda section. Immediately a picture came up of a panda climbing a tree. He looked so cuddly there

Giant Panda

was a chorus of "ahhs".

"He looks just like a teddy bear!" called Anna.

"Pandas *are* part of the bear family, Anna," said Miss Haynes, clicking on another picture of a panda sitting in the snow eating bamboo. "At one time people thought they were more similar to raccoons because of their black and white colouring but research has shown that they are definitely bears. So, what do you know about pandas, Emily?"

Emily grinned. "Lots!"

Miss Haynes, just like everyone in the class, knew that Emily was completely animal mad. She spent all her time reading animal books and magazines, drawing animals and looking at them on the Internet. "Well, they're very rare," Emily started to explain. "Only between one and two thousand are left in the world. They eat bamboo, but with the bamboo forests being cut down they have less food. And they sometimes get caught in traps that poachers set to catch other animals."

The class grew serious. "That's horrible," said Jack.

"Poachers should be stopped," said one of the other boys angrily.

Emily completely agreed. "WWF are trying to stop them," she explained. "They're creating reserves where the pandas can live. Places where they are safe and there's lots of bamboo – pandas eat for fourteen hours a day!"

"Wish I was a panda!" grinned Jack.

"You'd have to eat bamboo," Molly reminded him.

Jack pulled a face. "Oh yeah."

"That's all very

interesting, Emily," said Miss Haynes. "Now, why don't we have a look at some more pictures?"

A second later, a picture of the most adorable baby panda filled the whiteboard screen.

Everyone squealed.

"Maybe you'll meet a panda cub, Emily," said Molly.

"I'd have to be really lucky for that –
pandas don't have cubs very often so
they're very rare. Not only that, but pandas
are usually quite shy." Emily grinned.
"Knowing my luck, I'll probably just see
a whole load of panda poo!"

Anna pulled a face. "OK, maybe you're
not so lucky to be going after all!"

"Pandas poo a lot," Emily told everyone
enthusiasically. "When there are surveys of
pandas, the researchers have to pick up the
panda poo and look inside it."

There was a chorus of disgusted
exclamations.

"Gross!"

"Ew!"

"OK, Emily. I think that's enough
information for now," said Miss Haynes
hastily.

Emily sat down happily. She knew one
thing. She didn't care if she had to wade

through a *lake* of panda poo if it meant she got to see a real panda in the wild! She just couldn't wait for the summer holidays to start!

Getting Ready to Go!

"What did the panda say when he got stuck on the crossword?" Mike Oliver, Emily's dad, said, coming into the lounge.

"What?" Emily asked, looking up from her holiday packing list.

"I'm bamboozled!" Mr Oliver chuckled. "Get it? *Bamboo*-zled?"

Emily rolled her eyes. "Yes, all right, Dad, I get it." Her dad was always making rubbish jokes.

He ruffled her hair. "Looking forward to the trip then, love?"

"Oh yes!" she said. "I can't wait!"

Her dad grinned. "Your first trip outside Europe, and what a place to go to! You'll love seeing pandas in the wild. Mum and I are really pleased you can come with us."

Emily felt a bubble of excitement in her tummy at her dad's words.

"Now, where're my headphones? I need to brush up on my Mandarin." Mr Oliver spotted them attached to his iPod. "Ah, there we go."

Emily headed for the door. Her dad spoke very loudly when he was using one of his "learn-a-language" apps on his iPod. "I think I'll go to my room," she said, squeezing round the cases containing her

mum's cameras that were piled up by the
doorway.

She ran up the stairs and into her
bedroom. There was a large map of the
world on one side. Every other inch of wall
space was covered with posters of wild
animals, and a large cage from floor to
ceiling took pride of place at one end
of the room. Emily had a quick look in
but Cherry, her chinchilla, was in the
sleeping box.

She went across to the map. Running
her fingers over it, she found the place

they were
going to be
visiting – the
Minshan
Mountains.
Shutting
her eyes,
she thought

about the pictures she'd seen on the
computer at school that afternoon – tall
mountain peaks covered in cloud, dense
green forests, waterfalls, lakes of the
brightest turquoise ...

A chattering noise behind her made her
look round.

"Cherry! You made
me jump!"

Emily's chinchilla
was a soft round
ball of silver-grey
fluff. She had big
round ears, long
trembling whiskers, and
was about twice the size of a hamster. She
sat up on her haunches, chattering again.

Emily smiled. "OK, you can come out!"
She opened the cage door and imitated
the chinchilla's chattering sound. She loved
mimicking animal noises. Cherry hopped

out and ran up her arm. She stopped
on Emily's shoulder, her whiskers tickling
Emily's cheek. Emily sighed. Travelling
with her mum and dad was always fun,
but she hated leaving Cherry behind. Still,
their next-door neighbour would look after
her very well. Emily stroked Cherry's soft
fur and thought about China. Would a baby
panda's fur be as soft as this?

Oh, she prayed, *I hope I get the chance to
find out!*

The Minshan Mountains

The final weeks of term flew by and before
Emily knew it, there were only three more
days left of school, then two, and finally
their leaving date was upon them. They
were off!

It wasn't an easy journey – they had
to get on three aeroplanes and travel the
last section in a jeep. It felt very strange
to see all the road and shop signs written
in Chinese. Emily was very tired after
the flying but she forced her eyes to
stay open – she didn't want to miss a
thing. The driver of the jeep was called

Cheung Ming. He worked at the panda
reserve. He could speak a little English but
he didn't say much, concentrating instead
on the driving. There were lots of pot holes
in the roads and people were walking or
driving yaks. As they drove up into the
misty Minshan Mountains, Mr Oliver told
Emily all about the place they'd be staying.
It was a new reserve and had only
been open a few years.

"I was here when it started. Back then I
was working full-time helping set up new

projects," he said. "There were only five pandas in the reserve – a male, two females and two cubs. The adults all had GPS collars fitted so the research team could track them. Both females had cubs this year. The big question at the moment is whether any new pandas have moved into the reserve. The team think there could be more, but the reserve covers a huge area and pandas are very good at keeping themselves to themselves."

"I hope we find some new pandas while we're here!" Emily said eagerly.

Her mum smiled and put her arm round Emily's shoulders. "As well as looking for pandas you should keep an eye out for other animals and birds. There are so many amazing species here in this part of China – the golden eagle, the clouded leopard, golden monkeys ..."

"Is that why we've come?" Emily asked curiously. "So you can take photos and write articles about the different creatures?"

"Not exactly."

Her mum and dad glanced at each other.

"The main reason we're here is because of a problem in the panda reserve," Mr Oliver explained. "It's because of a rich businessman, Mr Chen."

There was an exclamation of disgust from Cheung Ming. "Mr Chen. Bad man," he said, shaking his head.

"Why's Mr Chen bad?" Emily asked her dad.

"He wants to build a large hotel complex on the edge of the reserve."

"It would be dreadful for the pandas," Emily's mum joined in. "They're shy creatures – all the building noise and hotel activity would be likely to make them leave the reserve."

"Aren't there laws against building right next to a reserve?" Emily asked in dismay.

"Not really," said her dad. "You see, Mr Chen is planning on building the hotel on an existing village. The villagers could object, but Mr Chen is claiming that the reserve isn't worthwhile because there aren't enough pandas living there. Mr Chen has also offered the villagers a lot of money to move out. The people here are very poor and they're bound to be tempted, even if it means them moving away from their homes. I just hope we can talk to them, persuade them not to let him build this resort."

"Your dad made a lot of friends here when the reserve was being built," Emily's mum explained. "The people might just listen to him."

Mr Oliver ran a hand through his curly hair. "It's not going to be easy though. Mr Chen is very persuasive."

Emily couldn't believe that anyone would just build a hotel if it put pandas at risk. "I hope you can stop him," she said.

Her dad nodded grimly. "I'm going to do all I can."

Just when Emily thought they couldn't travel any higher up the mountain, they reached the village that Mr Chen was targeting. There was a group of wooden houses with smoke drifting from makeshift chimneys. Children were playing in the

streets and a black yak
was being driven along
the side of the track,
its back piled high
with panniers.

"Wow!" Emily
gasped. It was like a
scene out of a history
book! They went through the village and
up to some metal gates. Cheung Ming
opened them and they drove into the
panda reserve.

A few minutes further on down the road,
they came to some modern white buildings.
The largest one, in the centre, had radio
antennae on the roof.

"The big building's the research base,"
explained Mr Oliver. "It's where we'll
meet with the team and eat. The smaller
buildings are where everyone sleeps."

They got out of the jeep and went to

the wooden building they would be staying in. It had a simple bedroom, a living room and a bathroom. There was a chest of drawers and a rail to hang clothes on, and cosy rugs on the floor. Emily's dad and Cheung Ming unloaded the cases. Cheung Ming carried Emily's bag into the house.

"*Xiexie*," Emily said, the word sounding like *share-share* as it came out of her mouth. It was one of the few words she knew in Mandarin – "thank you".

Cheung Ming smiled.

Emily sank down on her camp bed. She was exhausted! It was only late afternoon but she'd done so much travelling that her body wasn't sure if it was day or night!

"I think maybe you should just have a sleep, sweetheart," her mum said. "Get into your pyjamas. I'll stay with you, and Dad can go and say hi to everyone and catch up on what's been happening with Mr Chen."

"But I want to go exploring and meet people and . . . and . . ."

"Bed," Mrs Oliver said firmly. "There'll be time for everything tomorrow!"

Time to Explore

Emily blinked her eyes open. Looking up
at the unfamiliar wooden ceiling, she felt
confused, but as she sat up and saw her
mum and dad asleep in their beds next to
her, it all came flooding back. She was in
China! In the Minshan Mountains! Jumping
out of bed, she ran over to her mum. "Mum!
MUM! It's morning!"

"I'll get up in a minute, love," her mum
murmured sleepily.

Emily pulled on a T-shirt, hoodie and
jeans. "Can I go outside, Mum?"

"Yes, but don't go too far," her mum said.

"I won't!" Emily called, running outside.
She felt much better after a night's sleep.
The sun was just rising into the blue sky
and there was a delicious smell coming from
the research building. Her stomach gave a
growl. She couldn't *wait* for breakfast!

So, what to do? There was thick forest all
around her. She longed to go exploring, but
her mum had said she mustn't wander off on
her own. She looked around the buildings
for a while and then set off down the road
towards the village.

As she walked, she came across a girl,
crouching at the side of
the road. She was
slim, with straight
black hair to
her chin. Seeing
Emily, her eyes
widened. It was
clear she hadn't

expected to see a western girl. She smiled cautiously but in a friendly way.

Emily smiled back. "*Nin hao*," she said. *Hello.*

The girl started to talk swiftly. Emily spread her hands apologetically. "I don't understand. I'm sorry. My name" – she pointed to herself to help the girl understand what she was saying – "is Emily."

"Zhang Leung." The girl pointed to herself.

They grinned at each other.

"What were you looking at?" Emily pointed to the girl and then into the bushes, trying to mime what she was asking.

The girl said something in Mandarin. Emily had an idea. She held out her notepad and a pen.

Zhang Leung scribbled a picture. As Emily saw the round head and body, her eyes widened. "You were looking at a panda!"

Zhang Leung put her hand up to her eyes, as if she was looking for something, but then shook her head sadly. Emily thought she understood. The Chinese girl had been looking for pandas but hadn't seen one.

"Making friends, Emily?"

Hearing her dad's voice behind her, she looked round. Her mum and dad were coming towards them. Her mum had a camera slung around her neck.

"This is Zhang Leung," said Emily. "She was looking for pandas."

Her mum and dad spoke in Mandarin to Zhang Leung.

"You're right,"
Mr Oliver said
to Emily after
a few minutes.
"Zhang Leung
was looking for
pandas. She says
there have been
sightings of a
panda and her
cub nearby. She

thought she saw a flash of black and
white in the bushes as she was passing but
it disappeared."

"Isn't it rare for a panda to come so close
to humans?" Emily asked in surprise.

Her mum nodded. "It would certainly be
very unusual, so don't get your hopes up.
We'll probably have to go quite deep into
the forest before we find a panda – *if* we
find one at all."

Zhang Leung touched Mr Oliver's arm. She talked quickly, gesturing with her hands.

"Zhang Leung says that she's sure there is a panda nearby," he translated. "She found some fresh panda droppings through the trees over there. She lives in the village just outside the reserve and knows the research team are looking for pandas. She always keeps her eyes open. Maybe we should go and investigate?"

A small woman with a weathered face and grey hair escaping from a bun appeared on the path. "Zhang Leung!" she shouted, brandishing a pail.

"*Zai jian!*" the girl said to Emily and her parents. *Goodbye!* She ran off and was roundly told off by the old lady, who pushed the pail into her hands. Emily wondered if she was Zhang Leung's granny. She looked very fierce!

"So what now?" Mrs Oliver said, looking into the bushes. "Do you think there could be a panda nearby?"

"Well, it seems extremely unlikely," said Mr Oliver. "But if there's even a slight chance—"

"We should check it out!" Emily said excitedly.

Her mum grinned. "What are we waiting for? Let's go!"

Making Friends

The Olivers pushed their way through the tangle of bamboo to a small path. After about fifteen minutes of walking, Emily stopped. "Look at that!" She pointed to where some leaves and shoots had been torn away from the bamboo plants at the side of the path.

"That shows a panda's been here," said her dad. "See over there as well!" He went to where there were some scratch marks on a tree trunk. "Pandas leave

messages for other pandas who live nearby
— scratches on trees, scent markings, all
sorts of things . . ."

Emily spotted a mark
in the soft ground. It
looked like a big paw
print. "Look!"

"That's definitely a
panda print." Mrs Oliver
took the lens cap off her camera
and began taking photos. Emily noticed
another bush with leaves stripped off and
went over to investigate. As she did so, a
strange bleating sound echoed through the
trees. Parting the leaves, she pushed her way
through the bamboo to see what could
have made the noise. The sight before her
made her stop in her tracks. She sucked in
her breath, her heart beating faster.

"Mum! Dad! Over here!" she whispered.

"Oh my goodness!" her mum breathed

as they looked at the scene before them. It
was the perfect picture. On the other side
of the bamboo there was a clearing, and
in that clearing sat a giant panda, her legs
outstretched in front of her as she tore the
leaves off a stalk of bamboo.

"Don't look now but—" Emily's dad put
his hand on her arm.

Emily gasped as a cub came ambling
round from behind his mum with a rolling
side-to-side gait. He opened his mouth and

made a bleating
noise again.

Quietly, Mrs
Oliver picked up her
camera and started
to take photos. "The
cub's only about four
months old by the look of him," she said.

As she spoke, the cub tried to climb up
his mother's back and onto her shoulders,
but he soon lost his grip and rolled all the
way down to the ground. Luckily, his soft
fur cushioned the fall. He got to his feet,
looking surprised.

"Can we go closer?" Emily asked
longingly.

Mr Oliver shook his head. "Best not to.
It's not good for wild animals to get too
near to humans. If they get too tame it
could make them easy prey if any poachers
did come hunting."

"Oh." Emily was disappointed, but she knew that her dad was right.

"Look," whispered Mrs Oliver. "Can you see her GPS collar?" The mother panda had a dark collar around her neck, almost hidden by her thick fur. The panda must have heard them as, right at that moment, she stopped eating and looked over. She gave them a long thoughtful stare. Emily held her breath. She knew that pandas were really shy. Would the mother hurry off? But to Emily's relief, she clearly decided they weren't a threat and started munching on the bamboo cane again.

The cub came towards them, his eyes bright and inquisitive.

"What should we do?" whispered Emily as he came closer.

"Stay still. I'm sure he won't come too near to us," her dad said.

Emily held her breath. One step, two steps . . . before they knew it the cub was nearly upon them. He stopped just a metre away! Emily could make out the individual hairs on his black and white body and see his nose twitch. It was amazing!

He didn't look scared at all. He stared at Emily and then he bleated – "*Li-cccc-li-ccc*" – the sweetest sound. Emily couldn't resist – he looked so cute. She crouched down so she was at eye level with the little cub and made the same sound back at him. Suddenly the cub scampered forward and bounded onto her lap!

"Oof!" gasped Emily, toppling over backwards into the bamboo. The cub rolled off her. Emily sat up in astonishment. He wanted to be friends! Heart racing with excitement, she slowly held out her hand.

The baby panda sniffed at her fingertips and then put his large front paws on her knee before reaching up with his black nose. Touching her cheek, he snuffled at her ear.

"Hey, that tickles!" Emily giggled, and stroked the fur on his shoulders and under his chin. "You're gorgeous," she breathed.

The cub rubbed the side of his face against her hand.

"I think he likes you too," murmured her dad. "I've never known a wild panda be so friendly."

"I'm going to call him Li!" Emily grinned. "After the noise he made. Li . . . Li . . . you like that, don't you?" She tickled him under the chin.

By now the cub's mother had finished her bamboo and, as she got to her feet, she shook herself, before calling over her shoulder with a huffing noise. The panda cub backed away from Emily and trotted over to join his mum. Then they started to amble off into the trees.

"Goodbye!" called Emily, adding the same word in Mandarin. "*Zai jian.*"

The panda cub gave Emily one last look over his shoulder before going after his mother and disappearing into the thick tangle of bamboo.

Emily sank back onto her heels, her green eyes shining. "Did that really just happen?"

"It most certainly did! I've got the evidence right here," said her mum, fixing the lens cap back on her camera.

Emily glanced at her dad and saw that he was looking anxious. She suddenly felt guilty. "Sorry, Dad. I know I shouldn't have stroked him . . ."

"No, no, I'm not worried about what you did, Emily," Mr Oliver said quickly. "I'm just concerned that the panda cub and his mother are already so accustomed to humans. What will happen if this development goes ahead? They're so trusting that they could get too close to the people doing the building work and get seriously hurt."

"Oh, Dad!" Emily's mouth went dry as she thought about any harm coming to Li and his mother. "We can't let that happen. You'll have to convince the villagers to stop the development."

"I'll do my best," Mr Oliver promised.

Mr Chen's Plan

The Olivers headed back towards the research building for breakfast. Suddenly they heard the sound of a helicopter approaching. Emily's dad glanced up in surprise. "What's going on? There shouldn't be any helicopters flying over the reserve. It'll disturb the pandas."

"It must be tourists trying to get photos," said Mrs Oliver, frowning. "The pilot should know better!"

The black helicopter was almost above them now. The noise from the propellers was so loud; Emily put her hands to her ears. She felt as if the air was shaking. *Oh the poor pandas*, she thought, picturing Li and his mother. There was a red sword-like symbol on the helicopter doors and, in large letters, the words CHEN ENTERPRISES ran down its side. "Dad! It's not tourists!" cried Emily, pointing. "Look!"

"Mr Chen!" her dad exclaimed.

A man was taking photos through the helicopter window, using a camera with a long lens.

"What's he doing?" Emily asked.

Her mum lifted her own camera up to her eyes and zoomed in on the man in the helicopter. "It looks like he's using a heat-sensitive camera," she said as the plane flew over them. "It's a type of camera that is triggered to take a photograph whenever it senses heat given off by people or animals," she explained. "Cameras like that are great when used properly – we use them to take pictures of animal activity at night-time. They're attached to trees and the camera takes a photo whenever an animal passes by and records the time and date so researchers can use the information. But it's no good using heat-sensitive cameras from a helicopter. They can't penetrate through the canopy."

"So why was that man using one?" asked Emily, bewildered.

"I imagine Mr Chen must be trying to use the photos as proof that there aren't enough pandas here in the reserve to justify it being kept open. The villagers won't understand the technology and will just assume he's telling the truth."

"He'll probably offer to pay off those who do question it," said Mr Oliver. "From what the research team were saying last night, it sounds like he'll stop at nothing to build this resort."

"It would help if we could find real photographic evidence of new pandas living in the reserve," said Mrs Oliver. "The team have found droppings and panda markings that suggest there are new pandas here, but they haven't got any hard evidence as yet. If we can take some photos, then I'm sure the villagers wouldn't agree to sell up."

"We need to go looking for pandas," said Emily.

Her mum smiled. "That sounds like a good plan to me!"

Breakfast back at the research centre was nothing like Emily's usual breakfast of toast

and cereal. Instead they
had a clear vegetable
soup and some
warm steamed rolls
filled with chopped
vegetables and meat.
Emily's dad also ate a very spicy dish made
with peppers, but after one mouthful Emily
had had enough. She needed to drink a
whole glass of water! The rolls were delicious
though.

As she ate, her dad introduced her to
the research workers at the centre. As well
as Cheung Ming, there was an American
student called Lauren and a tall thin lady
called Dr Yuo, who was the zoologist
in charge of the team. There was also a
cheerful Australian vet, Brad Henson. They
were all fascinated to hear about Li and
his mother and, after checking the GPS,
told Emily that Li's mother was one of the

original pandas – an eight-year-old called
Mai Xiong.

"*May-Shong*," said Emily, repeating the
name as it sounded to her ears.

Dr Yuo nodded. "Now, if you could just
find us a few more new pandas, Emily, then
our problems would be sorted!"

"We're very keen to help you look," said
Mrs Oliver.

"Excellent! The more eyes the better,"

said Dr Yuo. "We thought we'd found one last week but the trail led down to the river in the ravine and just disappeared."

"And unfortunately, while we're looking, Mr Chen is getting more and more of the villagers on his side," said Brad.

"I'll try and help with that," declared Mr Oliver.

Later that morning, he set off to the village while Emily and Mrs Oliver headed back into the forest with Lauren and Brad. The sun was up, light slanting through the branches of the trees and striping the forest path. There were so many animals to see – little muntjac deer that bounded away with a strange barking noise, golden-haired monkeys that

swung through the branches above them, chattering and shrieking, and brightly coloured pheasants strutting through the undergrowth calling out to each other.

"It must be amazing working here all the time," Emily said to Lauren.

The American smiled. "It sure is. I just wish the pandas would show themselves more. I can spend days looking for them and not see a single one."

Emily began to realize just how lucky she'd been to see Li and his mum that morning – and how amazing it was that he'd been so friendly. *Oh, I hope I see Li again*, she thought longingly.

After several hours, they returned to the

centre. Emily was tired out from all the walking, and she sat down in one of the chairs in the research centre. Cheung Ming was working at a computer and the TV was on. On the screen, a man was being interviewed.

"Mr Chen," said Cheung Ming, pointing at the television.

"Mum!" called Emily. "Mr Chen's on TV!" She stared at the screen, wanting to see what Mr Chen was like. He was wearing a smart business suit and was smiling a lot at the interviewer but his smile didn't seem to reach his eyes.

Her mum came through and shook her head as she listened to the interview. "He's saying the reserve's a failure and that the new hotel will bring work and tourism into the area. He's being very persuasive."

Emily could see the interviewer nodding as if he agreed with everything Mr Chen said. She felt sick as she thought about the pandas and all the other wildlife in the reserve that would have to move away if the hotel was built.

"I hope Dad's managed to persuade the villagers not to sell," she said anxiously.

But when Mr Oliver arrived back later that day, he had a grim expression on his face.

"It's not good news, I'm afraid. Most of the villagers are convinced that there are very few pandas in the reserve, and they're very tempted to take the money." He sighed. "Some families are standing up to him – like the family of the girl you

met today – but most want to accept the
money and go."

Mrs Oliver's forehead creased into a
frown. "We'll just have to keep looking
for new pandas."

"We'll find some," Emily said. She met
her dad's worried eyes. "We have to!"

The following day, Emily, her mum, dad,
Brad and Lauren went deeper into the
reserve in the jeep. They looked and looked,
but once again they didn't see any pandas.
Tired and frustrated, they finally headed
back to the centre in the late afternoon.

Emily spotted Zhang Leung coming out
of the research centre talking to Cheung
Ming. She jumped out of the car to say
hi. Her new friend tugged at her arm,
motioning towards the forest.

"You think the pandas are nearby
again?" Emily said, understanding. "I'll ask

my mum if we can go
and look."

Mrs Oliver
nodded, and Emily
set off through
the trees with
Zhang Leung.
They went to the
clearing where Emily
had seen Li and his
mother the day before,
but it was empty. Emily's heart sank until
she spotted some fresh panda poo on the
ground.

"This way!" she said excitedly.

The two girls followed the trail of poo
and soon found Li and Mai Xiong in
another clearing. Li looked just as adorable
as he had the previous day, happily
clambering up onto his mum's lap.

"*Xiong mao.*" Zhang Leung pointed

excitedly. "Pan-da," she translated slowly.

Emily's heart was in her throat as she looked at the cub. Would Li remember her? She crouched down and made a soft bleating noise just like she had done the day before. Li didn't hesitate. He trotted straight over. Delight rushed through Emily. He *did* know who she was!

"Hello," she said as he climbed onto her knee. Looking round, she saw that Zhang Leung's eyes were wide. Emily beckoned her over.

The Chinese girl approached cautiously and knelt down. She held out her hand. Li sniffed at it and then climbed straight from Emily's lap onto Zhang Leung's knee.

Looking like she couldn't believe it, Zhang Leung stroked his fur.

The cub huffed at her in delight.

Zhang Leung giggled.

Li climbed back onto Emily's knee. She felt the heavy soft weight of him as he cuddled in to her. She kissed the fur on the top of his head protectively, her heart swelling with love.

"I'm going to save your home, Li," she whispered. "I promise."

Exploring the Ravine

Over the next few days, Emily, her parents and all the rest of the team did everything they could to find evidence of more pandas. But it wasn't until the fifth day that they had a real stroke of luck. Lauren had been out searching with Cheung Ming and had found some panda droppings among the thick trees near the ravine. A DNA analysis of the droppings suggested that they had been made by a panda new to the reserve.

"Oh, wow!" said Emily when she heard. "That's brilliant! Now all we have to do is find the panda and take photos."

But Dr Yuo was cautious. "The panda may have just been passing through the reserve. We need real proof that it is living here before we can try and stop Mr Chen."

At that moment, Emily's dad arrived back from another heated meeting in the village. "Things aren't looking good," he said, throwing himself into a chair. "Mr Chen has told the villagers they must agree to sell their houses by the end of the week or he'll withdraw the money he is offering."

"But that's only two days away!" exclaimed Mrs Oliver.

Mr Oliver looked worried. "I hate to say it, but maybe we should start planning to move the pandas we know are here in the reserve. In particular, Li and Mai Xiong."

"No!" burst out Emily. "We can't give up yet!"

"I don't want to give up either, Em," said Mr Oliver. "But we can't risk them being here when the diggers come in. Mr Chen will start the construction work as soon as the villagers have signed."

"But there might be a new panda near the ravine," Emily cried. "Can't we all go looking for it in the morning? The more people there are, the more chance we have of finding it." She looked from her dad to Dr Yuo. "Please, we have to try!"

Dr Yuo hesitated and then nodded. "All right, Emily. Tomorrow morning we'll all search. But if we find nothing then we must start making plans to evacuate the pandas."

Emily crossed her fingers. They had to find a panda the next day. They just had to . . .

The next morning the team gathered together outside the main building. Zhang Leung and her father had heard about the search and asked if they could help too.

Zhang Leung's father spoke to Emily. "Reserve good here. Hotel bad. Pandas will go." He pointed to himself and Zhang Leung. "We help look."

"Thank you." Emily smiled.

"Right, we're going to walk to the ravine," Dr Yuo instructed. "The forest is very dense there. Everyone should keep their eyes peeled for any signs of panda activity."

For the first hour, they walked along the familiar tracks through the bamboo, the tall slim stems reaching up all around them, the green leaves fluttering

as they passed. Emily and Zhang Leung
walked together, pointing things out to each
other – monkeys swinging through the trees,
and a small black, red and silver rose finch
watching them from a branch. Eventually
they reached a fast-flowing stream running
through the bottom of the ravine. On the
far side there was a steep slope covered with
a dense tangle of trees and bushes.

"That's where I found the droppings,"
Lauren said. "It's very hard to walk up the
slope though. The ground's slippery and
steep."

It did look hard, but Emily was
determined not to give up now. "Come on!"
she said. They crossed the stream, using the
rocks as stepping-stones, and set off up the

slope. Bamboo whipped against Emily's legs and feet, branches scratched at her and her feet slipped on the mud. By the time they had been fighting their way up the slope for half an hour, she was feeling very hot and sweaty and several times her mum had to catch her arm to stop her from falling.

Mrs Oliver gave Emily a worried look. "This is getting dangerous. I hadn't realized how steep it was going to be. Maybe I should take you and Zhang Leung back."

"No way!" Emily protested.

But just then, Zhang Leung tripped over. She cried out and clutched her ankle. Her dad crouched down beside her, talking anxiously in rapid Mandarin, as Brad examined it. "It's sprained," he said, taking

a bandage out of his kit bag. "It's not too bad but she should go home."

"I think Emily should go back too," said Mrs Oliver.

Emily opened her mouth to argue. "But—"

"No, Emily," her mum said firmly. "I know you want to help, but the team will be able to move faster without you."

Emily shut her mouth. She wanted to stay, but she didn't want to be a hindrance. "All right," she muttered. "I'll go back."

"Good girl," her mum said softly, squeezing her shoulder. "I'll come with you."

Once Zhang Leung's ankle was bandaged, the rest of the team headed on while Emily and Zhang Leung started back down towards the stream with Mrs Oliver and Zhang Leung's father. They had been walking for about ten minutes when a familiar noise echoed through the trees to the right of them. "*Li . . . cccc . . . li!*"

"It's Li!" Emily gasped.

"It could be another panda," Mrs Oliver said.

"No, it's definitely Li." Emily knew Li's call so well. Zhang Leung nodded too. "He must be through here!" Pulling the branches aside, Emily peered into the trees.

"*Li . . . cccc . . . li.*" The cub swung down from a branch just in front of her.

"Li!" Emily cried in delight. She fought her way through the bushes and came face to face with the little cub. As soon as Emily reached the branch, the baby panda climbed onto her shoulders. Emily heard Zhang Leung's dad exclaim in surprise. She grinned and dipped her shoulder down, tipping the cub into her arms.

He snuffled at her face and she kissed his nose, lowering him gently to the ground.

Zhang Leung's father spoke in Chinese to Mrs Oliver.

"I think he's saying he's never seen a panda do that before," Mrs Oliver translated. "It is very unusual!"

"Where's Mai Xiong?" wondered Emily.

Zhang Leung called something to her and pointed. Emily followed her friend's gaze and saw Mai Xiong dozing happily inside an old hollow tree trunk.

Li walked further into the trees. Suddenly he stopped, looked over his shoulder at Emily and made a yapping sound.

Emily had the strangest feeling that he was trying to tell her something. "What is it?" Li walked on a bit further, then stopped and yapped again.

Emily frowned. "I think he wants us to follow him, Mum."

Mrs Oliver smiled. "Don't be silly."

"No, he does. I'm sure of it!" Emily cried.

"Emily, wait! What about Zhang Leung's ankle?" Mrs Oliver looked round at Zhang Leung and her dad. "She can't walk through the undergrowth."

Her father spoke and pointed at Mai Xiong while Zhang Leung motioned them to go on.

"Well, they say they'll be happy watching Mai Xiong. All right. We'll go on a little way," Mrs Oliver agreed.

Emily was already up ahead, following Li as he made his way through the trees. The panda was far more nimble than her, climbing over tree stumps and pushing easily through the bamboo. He kept looking

back to see if she was behind him. Emily felt
sure he was taking them somewhere . . .

"What is it, Li?" Emily breathed. "What
do you want to show us?" She noticed that
the bamboo they were passing had been
chewed and scratched. A panda must have
been this way before them—

"Mum!" she gasped as they rounded a
corner and saw an incredible sight in front
of them. "Look!"

A Big Surprise!

A mother panda sat in a clearing. She was holding a very small panda cub. It was old enough to have fluffy black and white hair but was much smaller than Li. "Mum!" called Emily. "It's another baby panda!"

Mrs Oliver caught her breath. "Not just one, but two!" she cried as a second cub came pushing its way round its mother, bleating.

"Twins!" Emily beamed.

"And they both look equally healthy. This is incredibly rare!" Mrs Oliver's voice rose with excitement as she pulled the camera from over her neck. "Pandas often have twins but the babies almost never both reach adulthood. The mother usually only manages to look after one and the other dies within days of birth. But these two look really healthy. They must be about six weeks old from the size of them. This is amazing!"

She started clicking her camera, taking shots of the mother with the two adorable cubs. "And the mother has no collar on – that means she's new to the reserve. She must have made her home here before she had the babies."

Li came over to Emily and huffed softly, as if to say, *Told you I had something to show you!*

Emily crouched beside him and picked him up. "Thank you," she whispered in delight, kissing his fur.

As Emily held Li close, she watched the mother panda. She longed to go closer but she didn't want to risk upsetting her. It was enough just to see her nursing first one tiny baby and then the other as they squeaked and snuffled in her arms. It was the most amazing scene.

"This is perfect!" Mrs Oliver's eyes shone as she clicked away with her camera. "Just wait until we tell the others! A new panda

with twins, both babies doing well, and their
territory is within an hour's walk of Mr
Chen's proposed development. He'll never
be allowed to buy the land now!"

"So, this could save the reserve?" said
Emily.

Mrs Oliver smiled.
"Oh yes!"

Emily hugged
Li. She was
convinced he
had led them
there on purpose.

"You're really going
to miss Li, aren't you?" her mum said softly.

Emily nodded. She hated the thought of
leaving the little cub.

"It doesn't have to be goodbye for ever,"
her mum said. "Maybe we'll be able to
come back when he's older – I can always
try and arrange a photography trip."

Emily felt her sadness ease slightly. It would be amazing to come back when Li was bigger. Li started to struggle in her arms and she gently put him down. He gave himself a shake and then ambled off into the trees. Reaching the undergrowth, he looked back at her.

"Bye, Li," Emily whispered.

He huffed as if he were blowing her a kiss. Emily huffed back at him, and then the cub bounded into the trees.

Not goodbye for ever. Emily hugged her arms round herself. *Just for now.*

That night there was a massive celebration meal for everyone who had been involved in the day's expedition. While everyone in the team plus Zhang Leung and her dad feasted on delicious crispy chicken, vegetable rolls, noodles and rice, Mrs Oliver projected photos onto the white screen at the end of the room. When the final photo came up – a beautiful close-up of the mum feeding her twins – everyone cheered.

"Three new pandas living on the reserve!" said Dr Yuo in delight.

"And maybe more than that," announced Lauren, standing up. "I ran an analysis on some more droppings I collected today, and it suggests that there is another panda living in the ravine too. We'll find him or her and then that's *four* new pandas here!"

Everyone clapped and whooped.

"The reserve's safe!" said Mrs Oliver.

"It certainly is," Mr Oliver agreed, coming into the room, his phone in his hand. "I've just

Take a look at some of the pictures that inspired this story

A six year old male giant panda

Giant pandas in China

Giant pandas doing what pandas do best – eating bamboo!

The Yangtze is Asia's longest river, running through the Minshan Mountains in central China

White-handed gibbon (Hylobates lar) Image No: 109117 © Martin Harvey / WWF-Canon

It's not just giant pandas that live in China. These extremely rare white-handed gibbons are also found in the forests of south-east Asia.

Giant Panda (Ailuropoda melanoleuca) in a tree. Sichuan Province, China. Image No.: 113974
© Bernard De Wetter / WWF-Canon

Take a look at this acrobatic panda climbing a tree!

Giant panda (Ailuropoda melanoleuca), Sichuan Province, China Image No: 41598 © Fritz Pölking / WWF

Despite their size, giant pandas are very good at climbing.

had confirmation from Mr Chen's office –
he's announced he's dropping his plans for
the resort. Even if he could still persuade the
villagers to sell, which I doubt he could now
that they realize the reserve is a success,
he won't – the last thing he wants is to be
seen as the person responsible for chasing
incredibly rare twin babies from their home.
That wouldn't be good publicity for him
or his company at all! The photos have
saved the day. With that evidence, he's had
to give up."

Everyone cheered again, and then tucked
into sweet dumplings for pudding. There
was such a lovely atmosphere of friendship,
with everyone talking and laughing and
eating, Emily didn't think she'd ever felt
happier. She saw her dad looking through
her mum's photos and went over to him.

"Hey, Dad. I've got a joke for you," she
said, resting her head against his shoulder.

"What do you get if a load of pandas have a party?"

"What?" he said.

"*Panda*-monium!" Emily grinned.

Her dad chuckled. "That's worse than one of *my* jokes!" He put his arm around her. "You know, Em, I'm really glad you came on this trip. I'm so proud of you." He pulled her in tight. "You never gave up on the pandas. Not even for a second."

A warm glow spread from the tips of her toes to the top of her head. "I'd never give up," she announced, thinking of Li. "Not when there are animals in danger."

Her dad's eyes met hers and they smiled.

Emily hummed as she walked across her bedroom. It was the day after she had got back from China and she was feeling

particularly happy because Lauren had just
emailed to say that the other new panda
had been found – he was a young male.
She also said that the mother and twins
were doing well and
that she and Zhang
Leung had seen Li
and Mai Xiong in
their clearing.

Emily reached
up to stroke Cherry
who was perched
on her shoulder. It
was great to hear all
the news, but it was
also lovely to be back home with Cherry
again.

"So, what do you think?" Emily said,
holding up the photo she was carrying.
Cherry chirped. It was a print of Emily
with Zhang Leung and Li. Mrs Oliver had

given Zhang Leung the same photo before they left. Emily pictured Zhang Leung looking at it all the way across the world in China.

"Emily!" Her mum's voice called up the stairs. "Molly's here to see you!"

Emily stuck the photo to the map on her wall. She couldn't wait to tell Molly about all the new friends she had made!

Taking one last look at the photo, she smiled and ran out of the door.

Read on for lots of amazing panda facts, fun puzzles and more about WWF

Giant panda (Ailuropoda melanoleuca); Sichuan Province, China
China Project number: CN0005, Image No: 41632 © Fritz Pölking / WWF

Giant Panda Fact File

Best feature: Their distinctive black and white fur, of course!

Size: A giant panda usually measures about 150cm long (from nose to rump) and weighs 100–150kg.

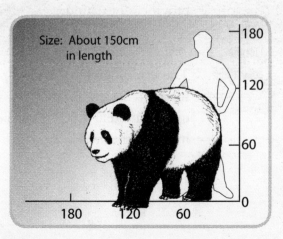

Size: About 150cm in length

Favourite food: Giant pandas are mega-munchers and spend over half their day (including night-time) eating! Bamboo makes up 99% of a giant panda's diet. They have to eat 12–38kg a day to sustain them – that's about the weight of you!

Home: The giant panda was once widespread throughout southern and eastern China, as well as neighbouring Burma and northern Vietnam, but can now only be found in twenty or so isolated patches of mountain forest in the Sichuan, Shaanxi and Gansu provinces of China.

Current population: The last official survey (carried out in 2004) counted approximately 1,600 giant pandas living in the wild.

Breeding and family:

In the wild, panda mothers usually give birth to a single baby – twins are more common with pandas in captivity. Their pregnancy lasts between four and six months, and when the panda cub is born it is 1/900th the size of its mother. This makes it one of the smallest newborn mammals compared to its mother's size – about the size of a stick of butter!

Life span:

A panda's average life span in the wild is 14–20 years, but giant pandas in captivity can live for up to 30 years.

Biggest threat:

The biggest threats to pandas are not predators in the wild, but everyday human actions. Their main problem is habitat loss, as more and more of their forest home is destroyed to make way for farms and new roads.

Bonus fact:

Giant pandas are excellent climbers and can swim.

Word Search

Reading across, up, down and diagonally,
see if you can find all the listed words
in the grid below ...

T	S	R	P	Q	P	O	W	Y	F	F	A	Z
E	N	D	A	N	G	E	R	E	D	B	W	J
L	W	C	N	C	F	L	M	N	R	P	I	B
I	E	D	D	G	H	K	N	E	I	H	L	I
F	B	E	A	H	J	I	M	N	E	A	D	H
F	N	A	I	H	C	A	N	I	D	B	L	H
X	B	T	M	H	B	E	F	A	C	I	I	G
Y	B	I	W	B	D	C	G	T	O	T	F	A
R	U	O	U	V	O	M	B	N	N	A	E	Z
S	T	N	W	E	N	O	Y	U	Y	T	O	V
X	S	T	X	L	K	J	C	O	O	U	I	Q
M	O	P	D	A	N	G	I	M	L	V	S	K
Q	C	O	N	S	E	R	V	A	T	I	O	N

PANDA	CHINA	HABITAT	WILDLIFE
ENDANGERED	BAMBOO	MOUNTAIN	CONSERVATION

Spot the Difference

Can you spot the five differences
between these two pandas?

Word Scramble

The names of these characters
from the book are all jumbled up.
Can you unscramble them?

MELYI

□□□□□

DRAB

□□□□

RO YUD

□□ □□□

LAGHEN ZUNG

□□□□□ □□□□

ROS MILREV

□□□ □□□□□□

Emily, Brad, Dr Yuo, Zhang Leung, Mrs Oliver

Feeding Time!

It's Li's dinner time! Can you lead him through the maze to the yummy patch of bamboo?

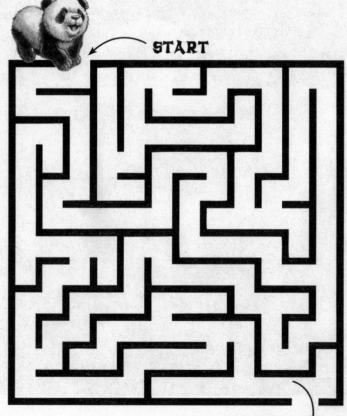

START

FINISH

Giant panda (Ailuropoda melanoleuca); Sichuan Province, China
China Project number: CN0005, Image No: 41625 © Fritz Pölking / WWF

More about WWF

WWF

You're probably familiar with WWF's panda logo, but did you know that WWF . . .

- Is the world's leading conservation organization.
- Was set up in 1961 (when TV was still black and white!).
- Works with lots of different people around the world, including governments, businesses and individuals, to make a difference to the world we live in.
- Is a charity and most of their money comes from members and supporters.

WWF's aim

The planet is our most precious resource and we need to take care of it! WWF want to build a future where people live in harmony with nature.

WWF are working towards this by:

- Protecting the natural world.

- Helping to limit climate change and find ways to help people deal with the impacts of it.

- Helping to change the way we live, so that the world's natural resources (like water and trees) are used more carefully, so they last for future generations.

Giant panda (Ailuropoda melanoleuca); Sichuan Province, China
Image No: 105347 © Michel Gunther / WWF-Canon

Giant panda (Ailuropoda melanoleuca); Sichuan Province, China
China Project number: CN0005, Image No: 41582 © Fritz Pölking / WWF

What do WWF do?

- **Conservation** – Protect rare species of wild animals and plants as well as important ecosystems found in forests, rivers and seas.

- **Climate change** – They don't just tackle the causes of global warming, but also the impacts of climate change on communities and environments.

- **Sustainability** – Help to change the way we all live, particularly in richer developed countries like the UK, including decisions about what we eat, buy and use for fuel.

How can I help WWF?

There are lots of ways you can take action in your own home to help protect our beautiful planet and the people and animals that live on it. Here are a few ideas to get you started . . .

Buy sustainable

One of the biggest threats to a lot of wildlife, including the giant panda, is loss of habitat. This is often from people cutting down trees to use in paper or wood products, or to make way for roads, and clearing areas to use for farming.

You can help stop this by only buying products that are sustainably farmed, or wood and paper products from sustainable forests.

So when you're out shopping with your mum or dad, look for:

- **Certified paper and wood products** (look for the FSC logo to tell if something is certified or not)

- **Products made from certified sustainable palm oil** (look for the RSPO logo to be sure that they are certified)

If your local shops don't stock these products – ask them why!

Reduce, reuse, recycle!

Households in the UK send 18 million tonnes of rubbish to landfill yearly. That's more than any other country in Europe!

Top five tips to reduce waste

Why don't you do some of these over a week and see how much less rubbish you throw away than normal?

Take a reuseable carrier bag when you go to the shops, instead of picking up a new one.

Take any clothes, shoes, books or toys you don't want any more to a charity shop.

Clean out old food jars and pots to use for storage.

Get creative with your rubbish and make a kitchen-roll penguin.

Make postcards by cutting old birthday and Christmas cards in half, and give them to your friends.

"Go Wild!"

The way we live can affect people, wildlife and habitats all around the world. Making small but important changes to the way we act really can help to save polar bears in the Arctic or orang-utans in Borneo and Sumatra.

And this is what the Go Wild club is all about. It's your chance to learn more about some of the animals and habitats that we're working to protect. It's also about discovering what you can do in your own home to help look after the natural world.

By joining WWF's Go Wild club at *wwf.org.uk/gowildjoin*, you will recieve a member's pack and magazines that will take you on an incredible journey around the world, meeting some amazing animals and individuals. You'll find out what life's like for them and the threats they face to their environments.

As well as getting lots of Go Wild goodies, being a member means that you help WWF to continue their work. Join today and explore your wild side!

Don't miss Emily's adventure with naughty tiger cub
Baalika in the next Wild Friends story . . .

Read on for a sneak peek!

Stripes

The ginger kitten peeped out from behind
the sofa. His green eyes were enormous in
his little face. "Here, Stripes." Emily knelt on
the carpet and approached her best friend
Molly's new pet. "Come on, don't be silly.
Come out." She edged closer but Stripes just
backed further behind the sofa.

Molly shot a worried look at Emily.
"How are we going to get him out? Maybe
I should go and find some food?"

"You don't need food," said Emily. "If
you want to get a kitten out from a hiding
place you just need to give him something

to chase." She looked round and saw an
old fluffy pink fairy wand that belonged
to Molly's little sister. "Watch this." Picking
it up, she moved the fluffy star along the
carpet near the sofa.

Stripes peered out. Seeing the moving
toy, his whole body stiffened and he
lowered himself down so his tummy was
almost touching the floor. Emily waggled it
invitingly.

Stripes couldn't resist. Springing out, he
started to chase the wand from side to side.
"See!" Emily grinned at Molly. She rolled
the kitten onto his back. He waved his paws

in the air, scrabbling with his little sharp
claws, and then jumped to his feet. "Here,
you try!"

Molly took the wand and moved it
around. Stripes chased it wildly, pouncing
and jumping. Molly giggled. "Why does he
like it so much?"

"All kittens love chasing things. It's their
way of practising their hunting skills for
when they're older," Emily explained. "Big
cats in the wild do it too."

"You know so much about animals,"
Molly said admiringly.

Emily smiled. She loved animals and was

always reading about them. It helped that her parents knew loads about them too. They worked for an organization called WWF that helped protect endangered animals. Emily's mum was a photographer and her dad helped to organize different WWF projects and wrote articles about them.

"Are you going away again this summer holiday?" Molly asked.

"Nope," Emily replied. "Mum's going to India tomorrow to take some photos in a reserve there, but as it shouldn't take long, Dad and I are staying behind."

"Cool, that means you can come round and play with Stripes lots," said Molly happily.

Emily grinned. She liked that idea!

"Well," Emily's dad, Mike Oliver, announced as they set off from Molly's house in the car a little while later. "I've just had some very exciting news. I've been asked to go to Borneo to write about an orang-utan reservation. I've got to fly out in a few days' time."

Emily stared at him. "Orang-utans! I'd love to see orang-utans in the wild!"

"I'm afraid you're not going to be able to come with me, love," Mr Oliver said, shaking his head. "The region I'll be staying in is quite unsettled, but" – his eyes twinkled – "how does a week in a tiger reserve in India sound instead?"

Emily stared at him. "You mean I get to go with Mum to India?"

Her dad nodded.

"Oh wow!" Emily gasped. *Tigers! She might actually see tigers in the wild!* "I'll have to phone Molly and tell her as soon as I get home!"

"And you'll need to pack," her dad said. "This time tomorrow you'll be at the airport, about to get on a plane!"

Emily was too excited to get to sleep that night. She'd put all the things she would need for her trip in her battered suitcase and it was now beside her bedroom door. As she lay in bed she listened to the familiar trundling sound of her chinchilla's exercise wheel. Cherry lived in an enormous cage in the corner of Emily's room.

Emily got up. It still wasn't properly dark outside and there was enough light for her to see. She undid the cage door. Cherry jumped out of her wheel, scampered up the branch that took up a big part of her cage and jumped out into Emily's outstretched hands, climbing up her arm to perch on her favourite spot – on top of Emily's head!

Emily stroked the chinchilla's soft grey fur. "I'm going away again tomorrow, Cherry," she said. The only bad thing about travelling all the time was having to leave Cherry behind, but her next-door neighbour was always happy to look after her.

Emily carried Cherry over to an enormous map of the world that she had stuck on one wall. Emily had pinned up a photo of an animal on every place she had ever visited. Most of them were in Europe, but on the right-hand-side of the map was a picture of a baby panda cub she'd met in China earlier that year.

"That's where I'm going tomorrow, Cherry." Emily pointed out India. Her heart quickened. "Imagine if I get to meet a tiger!"

The chinchilla squeaked.

Emily smiled. "All right, I can imagine you wouldn't like to meet a tiger!" She pictured a tiger in her mind, prowling around the forests of India. It would be amazing if she could see one in the wild!

Emily stifled a yawn and carefully encouraged Cherry to climb back into her hands. "OK, you can go and play some more," Emily said. "I really should try and get some sleep. It's going to be a long day of travelling tomorrow."

She put Cherry back in her cage. As she snuggled under the duvet she heard the exercise wheel starting up again. Emily shut her eyes and thought about tigers . . .

Lost in happy thoughts, she fell asleep.

**For more fun, games
and wild stories, visit
wwf.org.uk**